THE SPIDER BITES

MEDORA SALE

RAVEN BOOKS
an imprint of
ORCA BOOK PUBLISHERS

Library and Archives Canada Cataloguing in Publication

Sale, Medora
The spider bites / written by Medora Sale.
(Rapid reads)

ISBN 978-1-55469-282-8

I. Title. II. Series: Rapid reads

PS8587.A35387S65 2010   C813'.54   C2009-907250-5

First published in the United States, 2010
Library of Congress Control Number: 2009942218

Summary: Detective Rick Montoya must find out who firebombed his
apartment before he can clear his name of a bribery charge.

Orca Book Publishers gratefully acknowledges the support for
its publishing programs provided by the following agencies: the
Government of Canada through the Canada Book Fund and the
Canada Council for the Arts, and the Province of British Columbia
through the BC Arts Council and the Book Publishing Tax Credit.

Design by Teresa Bubela
Cover photography by Getty

ORCA BOOK PUBLISHERS   ORCA BOOK PUBLISHERS
PO Box 5626, Stn. B   PO Box 468
Victoria, BC Canada   Custer, WA USA
V8R 6S4   98240-0468

www.orcabook.com
Printed and bound in Canada.

13 12 11 10 • 4 3 2 1

For Harry,
as always

CHAPTER ONE

THE SPIDER COMES HOME

My name is Rick Montoya. Some people call me the Spider. But you don't have to. If you don't like spiders, you can call me Rick. I answer to both names.

It all started at sunset one day near the end of October. We had just come to the end of the late apple harvest. I had no reason to stay at the farm any longer. My boss, Scott, handed me a stack of fifty-dollar bills.

"Your pay, five months' worth. I deducted room rent and put the rest away. Just like you asked. Count it," he said. He tapped his finger on the pile of money. "Go on. Count it."

Scott's a nice guy. But not very friendly, if you know what I mean. I counted the money and divided it into four piles. I stuffed them into the pockets of my jeans. There was room for them all. With space for more. When I got home I was going to have to buy a new pair of jeans. These were much too big. I had already punched two more holes in my belt and it was still loose. I was a lot thinner than I had been when I started this job.

"I'm going into town if you want a ride," Scott said. "I can take you as far as the turnoff to the produce terminal."

I grabbed my backpack and climbed into the truck. It was time to get back to the city.

* * *

We didn't talk much on the trip in. I've known Scott all my life and he never did talk much, even as a kid. My father worked for his father. I grew up in a little house on the farm. When I was old enough, I worked for his father in the summers. So we knew each other. We didn't need words, most of the time.

"Where are you going?" he asked suddenly.

"Home," I said.

"Where's that?" asked Scott. "Angela's? Or your old apartment?"

"The old apartment."

"Why? What's there for you?"

I couldn't think of an answer to that.

"Look, if you're not going back to Angela, we'll just pick up your stuff. Then you can come back to the farm. I can always use you. It really helps to have someone in the crew who can speak Spanish. The workers seem to trust you."

"Thanks, Scott. I might need a job. But that'll be later."

"What do you mean?"

"I'm in a tight spot right now. You already know I'm under suspension until they wrap up this investigation. My lawyer says there's a good chance I'll be cleared. But then, he's paid to make me feel good, isn't he?"

"I hope he knows what he's doing," said Scott. And I think he meant it.

"So do I," I said. "Anyway, I've got something important to do first."

"What's that?"

"I have to find this guy, Freddie."

"Who's Freddie?"

"Just a guy."

He shook his head like he thought I was a little bit crazy, but he let it go.

Maybe I should have accepted his offer.

* * *

He dropped me off. I waved goodbye and started walking. It was three miles to the apartment, but that was nothing. Not after five months of hard physical work.

The long walk gave me time to think. It looked like I was through as a cop. Suspended from the force. Under investigation for corruption. Even if I got off on that charge, the slime would stick to me. I'd be fired and no one would hire me, even as a security guard. I had to face that, no matter how confident my lawyer was.

It was dark and cold out on the streets. It had been raining earlier. The sidewalks were wet and slippery, covered with fallen leaves. Even so, I reached West Central Avenue in under an hour.

Home was nearby. In an old house across from a park in a crowded, friendly neighborhood. The house had three stories and a basement, and had been divided into three apartments. I rented the basement. It had its own entrance at the side. I liked that. And it was quiet. It felt safe and private. A fox or a rabbit would be happy hiding down there. Or a spider.

The apartment was supposed to be empty. Before I left, I had paid my landlady, Cheryl, the rent for six months. But there were lights on in the kitchen and the living room.

The street was deserted because of the rain and the cold. I walked cautiously down the driveway between the house and its next-door neighbor. The automatic security light went on. That didn't bother me. It goes on when a cat walks by. Or a raccoon.

I stopped and listened for signs of movement. Everything was quiet. I went around to the back window. I could see into the brightly lit kitchen. It was empty. Then I bent down and looked around. There were dirty pots on the stove and dishes stacked in the sink. Through the kitchen door, I saw a shadow move. The hall light went out. Then a hand reached into the kitchen and turned out the light.

CHAPTER TWO

FIRE

I took a step sideways from the window. For a minute I stood still, listening. The person in my apartment didn't move. He hadn't broken in. He was living in my apartment. At least he was cooking and eating there. I took out my key and went back to the side door. The key didn't work. Cheryl had rented my apartment to someone else, and I had scared the hell out of him. Or her. I swore under my breath.

The last thing I wanted tonight was a fight over the apartment. I wanted a bed and a shower and a little peace and quiet. I'd sort it out tomorrow.

I walked back up to West Central and took a room at the nearest hotel.

* * *

I crawled into bed and slept until six the next morning. Hunger woke me up. I hadn't eaten since lunch the day before.

It was too early for breakfast. The closest place for a decent breakfast was the Coffee Corner. It opened at seven. My landlady worked the morning shift there. Naturally I wanted to talk to her about who was living in my apartment. But I really didn't want to argue about it over my pancakes and coffee.

I took a long shower to fill the time. Then I went out. One of those coffee franchises had moved in right across the street from the Coffee Corner. It was already open. So there I was, sitting on an uncomfortable stool, eating a stale muffin and drinking warm, flavored water. I thought of Cheryl's pancakes and strong, hot coffee. What else could I do? I'd go back and talk to Cheryl after she got off work. Anyway, I had other things to look after.

I had left town in mid-May. I stopped shaving in June and let my hair grow. Seeing myself in the bathroom mirror after my shower that morning, I realized I now looked like the Wild Man of the Woods. I needed a major cleanup. Then I needed some clothes that fit me.

* * *

"Why not keep the beard, Rick?" asked my barber. "I'll trim it for you. See how you like it."

I nodded. "Whatever you think, Vito," I said. I didn't care how I looked right now. Up to a point. But I had to look respectable and clean. I closed my eyes and let Vito wash and cut and trim. My mind was on what I was doing back in town.

Getting into my apartment was the least of my problems. I wondered if it was possible to get my job back. After all, right now, I was only suspended. I hadn't been fired. Yet. Did I want my job back? I had to decide if I wanted to face the guys I used to work with. Especially since most of them believed I was on Rodriguez's payroll. That had nothing to do with the way my hair looked.

"What do you think, Rick?"

I opened my eyes. "About what, Vito?"

"The beard. If I shave it off, your chin will look pretty funny. You've got a real dark tan on the rest of your face. Your chin will be white."

"Leave it then," I said. "It doesn't matter."

I left Vito's, feeling much neater, and strolled along West Central to George's Menswear. It had good stuff. Nothing fancy and nothing too expensive.

I was looking through a rack of trousers a little smaller than my old ones.

"Those trousers are going to be too large for you, sir," said the salesman. "Try these." He handed me an impossibly small pair.

"I won't get into those," I said.

"Try them on, sir," he insisted.

I came out of the dressing room and looked in the mirror. A bearded stranger looked back at me. I hadn't been that thin for fifteen years. Not since I was twenty. The sun had turned my face into leather. But the pants fit.

"I'm in a hurry," I said. "I need these right away."

"Can you give us an hour to do the cuffs?"

"I can if you can find me a pair of jeans to wear right now," I said. "And I'll come back for these after lunch."

I needed to look good enough to buy a decent lunch. And maybe even go and see my lawyer. I was hungry, dammit. I wanted food. I wanted a place to live and a job. And my good name back. Maybe that would even give me…What? What else had I lost?

My wife. She wasn't going to be as easy to replace as a pair of pants.

* * *

It was four o'clock before I was walking back down the street toward my apartment. I was ready to have a talk with Cheryl.

A siren screamed behind me. Then another one. First a fire truck tore past, then an ambulance and two police cars. Another fire truck followed them. Not a routine call, I thought automatically. Something big had happened.

Then I saw the flashing lights. There were already cars parked down the street. The vehicles that had passed me were second and third backup units. There were too many emergency vehicles to fit on the street. The air was full of smoke.

There was a crowd on the sidewalk ahead of me. Two men in uniform were trying to hold it back. I crossed the street to the park and stood beside a tree. The air stank of burning furniture and water on charred wood. And worse things.

The wind rose and blew some of the smoke away. I could see what was going on. Across the street was my old house. I'd lived there for three happy years. Then I'd gone back to it in December, when Angela threw me out. To hide and lick my wounds. It was the closest thing I had to a home.

Two paramedics were carrying a body bag on a stretcher. Someone had died in the fire.

CHAPTER THREE

SUSANNA

The paramedics pushed the stretcher into an ambulance. The driver yelled at someone. I could see his problem. He was stuck. There was a fire truck in front of him and three police cars beside him. Men in uniform were standing around, doing nothing. He walked from group to group. At each one he pointed at his vehicle. It was almost funny, but it wasn't.

Five minutes later the fire truck left. The cops in uniform climbed into their cars. They turned around and left. Things were winding down.

The ambulance made its way around the remaining vehicles. It drove off at a slow, steady pace. Its emergency lights and siren were off. There was no need to hurry. It was going to the morgue, not the hospital. The streetlights came on. It was beginning to get dark. The crowd started drifting away. Only a handful of curiosity seekers were left. What were they hoping to see? More bodies?

A woman came running up the street toward the house. Her black coat flapped behind her in the wind. Her hair was blowing across her face, getting in her eyes. She saw the little crowd of people and slowed down, gasping for breath. She pushed back her hair and bent over. Someone from the emergency team walked over to her and patted her shoulder. She straightened up and said something. He shook his head.

The streetlight was shining full on her face now. It was Susanna, Cheryl's daughter. But where was Cheryl? I hadn't seen her in the crowd. She should have been home by now. Maybe she was next door. Susanna buried her face in her hands. The man patted her shoulder again. She moved away from his touch and reached into her pocket for a tissue. Then she turned and stared at the remains of the house.

What she was thinking? Poor Susanna. The building had been her home for all twenty-six years of her life. There wasn't much left of it now. I started walking toward her. I needed to find out what had happened. But I stopped. What she needed was someone to comfort her. This was not a good time for asking questions.

I slipped away before she saw me.

*   *   *

I walked into the hotel and headed for the elevator. But what was I supposed to do in my room? Sit on the bed and watch television? I turned and went into the bar. In this neighborhood late afternoon was a dead time for selling beer. The bar was almost empty. Four men were sitting at a round table whispering to each other. Setting up a deal, I thought. But it wasn't my business. Not at the moment. The waitress came by carrying a jug of cold draft and four glasses on a tray. It looked good.

"Coffee," I said. "And a glass of water." I wanted to keep a clear head.

The television above the bar was set to the local news channel. Half the screen flashed pictures. Another section was giving the local traffic report. But with no sound, none of it made any sense. The waitress set down my coffee and glass of water.

"Two-fifty," she said.

I dropped a five on her tray. She reached for change.

"It's yours," I said. "And could you turn up the sound?"

"Those guys asked me to turn it down," she said.

"I'll move closer. Just turn it up a bit."

"You're the boss," she said.

I moved to the table next to the bar. I was just in time for a Breaking News flash. An excited-looking young reporter was standing on the street outside Cheryl's house. She pointed at the ruins and told us the house was beyond saving. Then she tried to get the neighbors to talk.

"It's terrible," said one.

"Was there someone in the house?" asked the reporter, looking around.

"Dunno," said the first neighbor.

"The owner," said someone else. "Poor woman."

"Did you know her?" asked the reporter.

"Everyone knew Cheryl," said another. "Sort of."

The reporter smiled, nodded and turned to the camera. "The fire that may have killed the popular woman who lived in this house started between two thirty and three this afternoon. One neighbor has told me that she heard an explosion. Whatever might have caused the fire, the house is beyond repair. We know that at least two bodies have been recovered from the ruins. Their identities are being withheld until their families can be notified. The owner of the house is believed to be one of the dead. The second victim may be a tenant who lived in the basement apartment."

"Thanks," I said to the waitress and stood up. "You can turn the sound off again if you want."

* * *

I figured Susanna would still be somewhere around the old neighborhood. One of her friends or her mother's friends would have taken her in. I headed back to the site of the fire.

I stopped on the sidewalk to check things out. Three men were setting up huge outdoor lights. New teams of firemen and police were poking through the rubble.

Susanna was standing on the porch of a house two doors away. She was clutching the porch railing. She was so still she looked like a statue. Her eyes were fixed on the men working in the ruins. I walked over to the porch stairs.

"Hi," I said.

She turned her head and looked straight at me. There was no expression at all on her face. I don't think she even saw me standing down there.

"Susanna," I said. "It's me, Rick. I just heard about the fire. I'm sorry. Is there anything I can do?"

She stared at me.

"My god. Rick? Is that you? But you were killed in the fire!"

CHAPTER FOUR

THE MAN IN THE BASEMENT

"Of course it's me," I said. "Who else?"
She moved over to the top of the stairs to get a better look.

"You've changed. You look different."

"That doesn't matter," I said. "Listen, Susanna, I'm worried about you. You can't just stand on the porch out here in the dark."

"What am I supposed to do?"

I didn't have an answer to that. "I have to talk to you, Susanna."

"About what?" she asked.

"What have they told you about the fire?"

"Nothing, Rick. And I'm going crazy.

They won't tell me anything. I'm so scared."

She looked cold, standing there on the porch. She was shivering. I had to get her into someplace warm. Right now.

"No need to be scared," I said. "Come on, Susanna. Come with me. Let's go grab a pizza."

*　*　*

We walked back toward the familiar, comforting sound of traffic going home. It was getting to the end of rush hour. We reached West Central, and Susanna seemed to relax a little.

The pizzeria was crowded with people waiting for takeout. I found us a quiet table at the back and ordered a large pepperoni pizza with extra mushrooms.

"Is that okay?" I asked.

"It's what I always have," said Susanna.

"I know. I remembered," I said. "But people change."

"I don't," said Susanna.

"I guess not. You never did like change, did you? Even as a kid."

She stared across the table at me.

"I can't get over how you look. What happened?"

"Nothing much," I said. "I've been on a farm. Working hard. I lost some weight and grew a beard. It's still me. You look different too."

She glanced down at her outfit. She was wearing a red dress and expensive-looking brown boots. She had tied a brown and red silk scarf around her neck. There were blond and silver streaks in her dark hair, and her face was covered in makeup. She looked like a model. I was more used to seeing her in jeans.

"Oh," she said, "I just had my hair done. I had a date tonight." Her eyes filled with tears. "It seems kind of stupid to be dressed like this now."

"Don't worry about it. Tell me about the fire."

"I can't. I don't know anything. I was at work today."

"How is the job going? Are you still working at 52 Division?"

"Yeah," she said. "It's going well. I've been meaning to thank you."

"What for?"

"Recommending me for the job. All the guys there are really nice."

"You like cops?" I asked, trying to smile.

"Most of them," she said. "Anyway, like I said, I had a date. So I took the afternoon off to have my hair done."

"You got dressed like that to have your hair done? Do you have to do that?"

Her cheeks turned red under her makeup. "Of course not. I put it on before I left work. I thought maybe I wouldn't have time to go home and change. Anyway, it was almost five o'clock before I got back to the station. They told me about the fire."

"And you came over."

"They told me Cheryl was dead, and I came over."

The waitress set the pizza down on our table. Susanna stared at it. Like she had never seen pizza before.

"Help yourself," I said, pushing it closer to her. But my mind wasn't on pizza. I was wondering why she always called her mother by her first name. I had asked her that once before, and she had laughed. "Cheryl thinks we're like friends. Not like mother and daughter," she had said.

I still wondered.

She pulled off a wedge of pizza and took a bite.

"It's too hot," she said. She waved it in the air to cool it down. "You know, all the way home, I kept thinking I had to cancel my date. After spending all that money for my hair. And getting my makeup done too. And my nails. I even had to take a half-day off work without pay."

I must have looked shocked. She shrugged her shoulders.

"Stupid, eh? It's funny the weird things that go through your head like that."

"Was the date something very special?"

"No. Just dinner and a movie. But I was really looking forward to it. And instead, here I am, eating pizza." She took a huge bite, swallowed and then took another huge bite.

"With me. Sorry about that." I tried to think of something better to say. I couldn't.

So I sat and watched her finish off the second slice as fast as the first one. I've had to tell a lot of people that someone very close to them had died. The bad news takes them in different ways. Some scream and cry. Some reach for the liquor bottle and get drunk. Others just go still. Like they were frozen inside. But I'd never come across someone who ate pizza and talked nonstop. It was weird. Maybe other people do that too. I don't know. It takes all kinds.

I didn't ask her about it.

"Why did you say you were scared?" I said.

"Did I say that?"

"Yeah. On the porch. You said you were scared."

She blinked and took another piece of pizza.

"Well—wouldn't you be scared? I mean, I could have been home. I would have died in the fire too. Maybe someone wanted to kill us both."

"But whoever it was must have known you'd be at work," I said.

"I guess. But then they told me that you'd been killed too. You and Cheryl. There were two bodies. And here you are. If the second one wasn't you, who was the man in the basement?"

CHAPTER FIVE

ALONE

"This is so weird," said Susanna, taking another slice of pizza. "If you hadn't come back today, we would have buried that guy, thinking he was you. Who was he anyway?"

I shook my head.

"I don't know who he was, Susanna."

"You mean we'll never know?"

"I didn't say that. These crime-scene guys are geniuses at sorting out burnt and fragmented evidence. They'll probably have a confirmed ID in a matter of days. But you must have known it wasn't me in the apartment."

"Not really. Of course I noticed someone had moved in a few days ago. But I lived on the third floor," she said. "And I'm at work all day. I didn't know who it was. I asked Cheryl. She said it was none of our business. It was your apartment. You could do what you like with it."

"She did?"

"Yes. I thought maybe you were hiding out down there. Weren't you wanted for questioning?"

"Listen, Susanna. Everyone knew where I was. I wasn't hiding. They knew how to reach me, night or day. Cheryl, the guys at 52 Division, the big brass running the investigation. Everyone."

"You weren't hiding?"

"No."

"So why did you leave?"

"I wanted to get away for a while," I said. "Cheryl knew that."

"She didn't tell me," said Susanna, frowning. "But I can't believe she'd lie to me."

"And you never saw the man in the basement?"

"No," she said slowly.

"And you never heard anything?"

She glanced up at me.

"Well...I thought I overheard Cheryl call him Fred."

"Really?" I said. "Are you sure?"

"No, not completely."

"But you still thought it might be me down there?"

"I thought maybe it was one of her jokes. I mean, calling you Fred. Then I wondered if he was a new boyfriend. She could have been sleeping with him. I don't know. She never talked about her private life."

"I really don't think Freddie was Cheryl's kind of guy, Susanna."

"How would you know? What did you ever know about her? God—men can be so stupid." She spat the words out.

"I guess we can be," I said. "Sometimes. But Cheryl..."

"Look, Rick. I don't want to talk about her, okay? Not tonight."

"No problem," I said. "Are you going to be all right?"

"I guess so. But the guys at work are betting on it being arson. And they wanted to talk to me. Do they think I had something to do with it?"

"Come on, Susanna. Of course they don't," I said. "But you know more about Cheryl and the house than anyone, don't you?"

"I guess."

"So they have to talk to you. Did you stay and talk?"

"No! I said I was going over to the house and I left. Do you think they're mad at me?"

"Of course not," I said. That was a lie. Those guys weren't very good at sympathy. Still, it wasn't my problem. "It can wait until tomorrow."

"I hope so."

"Why do they suspect arson?"

"I don't know," she said. "They didn't say. So where are you staying? With Angela? I see her around sometimes. I guess she hasn't moved."

"No," I said. I didn't feel like talking about Angela with anyone. Especially not now.

"Are they going to prosecute you?" she asked, picking at her fifth slice of pizza.

"I don't know," I said.

"I asked Tony. He said they were still going over the evidence. I guess this fire really screws up the investigation."

"Why would it?" I said. "They've been through my apartment enough times already. They found everything that was down there."

"Are you sure?"

"If there was something there, they found it."

"Tony thought you were innocent. Probably."

"Why?" I asked. I was curious.

"He said you're too smart to stuff twenty thousand dollars under your mattress.

Only a total idiot would do that. And you're not a total idiot."

"Nice," I said.

"Is that why the guys call you the Spider?" she asked. "Are spiders supposed to be clever?"

I shook my head. "Ask the guys," I said. "They know more about it than I do."

"I did. They wouldn't tell me. It's such an awful name. I hate spiders."

"Sorry. And I appreciate Tony's support. But not being dumb enough to hide money under my mattress is not evidence. Even clever people do stupid things sometimes."

"So—was it money they gave you?"

"For the record, Susanna, love, no one paid me off. It was a frame. I was getting too close to them. They wanted me off the investigation."

"I guess it worked, didn't it?" said Susanna. "Too bad."

"Sure," I said. "In real life, the bad guys win once in a while. Some of them win all the time. But it doesn't explain why someone wanted to burn down your mother's house."

Susanna shook her head. Her expensively streaked hair gleamed as it moved.

"I haven't got the faintest idea," she said.

"I don't either," I said. "It doesn't make any sense, unless…"

"Unless what?" she said quickly.

"Nothing. Just a few stupid ideas going through my clever head."

"I better go, Rick," said Susanna. "No one knows where I am, and I'm pretty tired."

"Do you have someplace to sleep for the next few days?" I asked.

"I'll be at Jenny's." Jenny lived next door to the old house.

"Good," I said.

"She's going to lend me jeans and stuff. This dress is all I have now. Everything else is gone." She looked suddenly grief-stricken.

"Don't worry, Susanna. We'll find out who did it."

"You will? How?"

"A lot of evidence is left behind after a fire. People think everything gets burnt.

It doesn't. They'll find out who did it."

She stood up abruptly. "I have to go."

"Wait," I said. "How can I get in touch with you?"

She picked up a clean paper napkin and scribbled a number on it.

"My cell," she said and ran out of the pizzeria.

CHAPTER SIX

LOOKING BACK

B ack in the hotel, I was stretched out on the bed, thinking. A jumble of ideas ran around in my head. But none of them fit together. How well did I know Susanna? Her behavior tonight surprised me. But she was an adult now. People change.

When I first met her, she was about ten. I had just started with the police department. I was a raw recruit, scared to death of doing something wrong. And I needed a place to live.

I walked up and down the streets near the station, looking for a room. I saw a sign in a window. *Basement apartment.*

Partly furnished. Reasonable rent. That sign was pure Cheryl. She believed in telling the truth. The apartment was in the basement and the rent was low. But it had its own kitchen, a bathroom with a shower, and one more big room. It had a couple of chairs and a couch in it. And there was a comfortable bed in the corner.

We sat in the kitchen and talked. Cheryl was in her thirties, shy and pleasant. I was just a kid, shy and nervous. We found each other easy to talk to. Her husband had died three weeks before. She was still in shock. But she had gone out and found a job as a waitress. Now she wanted to rent out the apartment. She needed the extra money. "Anyway, the house is too big just for me and my little girl." She pulled out a tissue and blew her nose. "Sorry," she whispered.

I liked her and the apartment. Cheryl liked the idea of having a cop in the basement, even a young one. We got along just fine for the next few years. It was not a happy household in those early days. Cheryl was struggling to cope with her grief. And her daughter's unhappiness. The first thing Susanna told me was how much she missed her father.

"He loved me more than anyone else in the whole world," she said. "He did. I know it." She sounded angry.

"Of course he loved you," I said. "But surely he loved your mother just as much."

"He liked her okay," said Susanna. "But it was me he loved."

I remember being shocked, then thinking, Poor little kid. She's young. She's upset. She'll get over it.

Now I lay there, wondering if she had.

* * *

I was sure that Susanna was wrong about one thing. Cheryl could not possibly have been having an affair with Freddie. It didn't seem possible. Freddie was a sewer rat.

I used to tease Cheryl about finding some rich, handsome guy at the Coffee Corner. She would shake her head. She always said that she was too busy for a lover. I had breakfast there almost every day. All the regular customers loved her. But she was attracted to the quiet, serious ones. Those were the guys she would sit with on mornings when it wasn't busy, talking to them about all kinds of things. Not to a loudmouth like Freddie.

Then I met Angela. She had just been posted to our division. She was lively, funny, clever and beautiful. We fell in love. We found an apartment not far away and moved in together. Soon after that, we got married. But we still had breakfast at the Coffee Corner.

That was before Freddie moved into my life. And destroyed it.

* * *

After kicking these ideas around in my head, I picked up my cell phone. Susanna answered on the first ring.

"It's you," she said. I couldn't tell if she was pleased or disappointed. Most likely, she just didn't care right now.

"Are you at Jenny's?" I asked.

"Where else would I be?" she said. "Look, I'm sorry. We're going to bed. I'm really tired."

"I'm not surprised," I said. "I just want to let you know that I'm going over to the house. There are some things I need to check out. So if you see a flashlight moving around, don't freak out. It's just me."

"Why do that?" she asked.

"You know, Susanna, maybe someone was out to kill me. I'd like to know who the hell he is," I said. "I think the easiest way to find out is to go over there and look around."

"That doesn't make sense, Rick," she said.

"It does to me. Good night, sweetheart. Try to get some sleep. I'll call you tomorrow."

"What do you expect to find?"

"Nothing, I hope. Nothing at all. And that would make me very happy."

I changed into a pair of jeans, my new heavy shirt and an old warm sweater. I slipped a big flashlight and a bottle of water into my backpack. Last of all I put on my steel-toed work boots and picked up my jacket. I was ready for a long night.

CHAPTER SEVEN

THE CRIME SCENE

A bright bluish light surrounded the burned-out house. Like something from a sci-fi movie. But there weren't any creatures from outer space on the scene. Only a small crew of crime-scene investigators. And a few bored-looking uniformed cops. Right now the CSI guys were crawling through the rubble. One of them raised his arm.

"Hey, Chris, I found another one," he called.

"Good," said someone. "Mark it and I'll put it with the rest."

Another what? I wondered. What exciting things were they finding? The melted remains of my old toothbrush, maybe? Pieces of my coffee pot? I was in the park across from the house. Most of the emergency vehicles had left. The CSI team's white van was sitting in the neighbor's driveway. I had a clear view of what was going on. Not much.

A few people walked down the street and stopped to stare. None of them stayed long. It really wasn't very interesting. Unless it was *your* life they were pawing over. I was interested.

Then a woman came along. She was moving fast, taking long strides. But she wasn't hurrying. Just walking like someone I used to know. Someone who loved taking long walks. Then the woman stopped in the pool of light from the powerful lamps and looked around.

My stomach lurched. I sat down on a park bench, stunned. It was the last thing I expected. I took a deep breath and stood up again. She must have seen me move out of the corner of her eye. She turned her head and looked straight at me. It really was Angela. The full force of how much I missed her hit me. She was standing in harsh light. She had on a pair of baggy pants and my old thick red sweater. She looked unbelievably beautiful. And desirable.

But she didn't recognize me. How could she? It was dark where I was standing. Half my face was hidden behind a beard. My body was half as wide as it used to be. I don't think anyone had recognized me at first sight. In one way, I was glad. But it still hurt. She turned back and walked toward the team.

"Hey, Tony," she called. "Mark. I'm over here."

Tony Marchetti, my old partner and closest friend—except for Angela—stepped out of the shadows by the house. He was talking to a tall guy. I didn't recognize him.

"Thanks for coming out, Angela, sweetheart," said Tony. His familiar voice rang out in the dark. "Sorry it's such a lousy night."

They moved closer to each other. I got a good look at the other man as he walked under the light. Their voices dropped.

I couldn't hear what they were saying. I couldn't hear anything but my heart pounding. I moved out of the park toward them. Halfway across the street I heard Angela's voice.

"The hell he is," she was saying.

She stepped aside. Tony was staring intently at me. I turned and walked away from them, back to the park, feeling as if I'd just run ten miles.

* * *

When I looked again, Angela seemed to be arguing with Tony. He shook his head. She said something to the other guy and started back up the street. When I looked again, the second man had disappeared. I followed behind her, sticking to the edge of the park on the opposite side of the street. She stopped, suddenly, halfway between the ruined house and the bright lights and traffic.

"Come here," she said. "I want to talk to you."

I walked across the street, feeling stupid.

"You recognized me," I said.

"Of course I recognized you," said Angela. "I lived with you for ten years. I worked with you for even longer. How could I not recognize you?"

"As far as I know, no one else has," I said. "They can't see past the beard. And I've lost weight."

"So you have. But you still walk the same way. You still hold your head the same way when you're listening. You're still you, dammit."

"Why did you come down here?" I asked.

"They called me. They said you were dead. It wasn't nice," she said. She turned her head away. "I had to go to the morgue to identify you."

"I'm sorry, Angela. They shouldn't have made you do that. Anyway, it wasn't me."

"I know that," she said. "The body wasn't exactly recognizable. But the watch and scraps of clothes weren't yours. And you've never worn a gold neck chain. Not that I've seen anyway."

"But you didn't have to come down here," I said.

"Tony asked me to. And I'm still down as your next of kin, along with your dad."

"He's in Costa Rica."

"I told them that. Then they said that Tony was here at the house. He wanted to talk to me. So here I am."

"What did he want?"

"Besides asking if you were dead? Nothing. I told him it wasn't you in the morgue. Anyway, by then I'd seen you. For a cop, you're not very good at discreet surveillance, are you?"

She sounded very, very angry.

"I've lost my edge," I said. "Did you tell him I was in the park?"

"Why would I do that?" she asked.

Why wouldn't she? I wondered. And that puzzled me even more.

CHAPTER EIGHT

ANGELA

We started walking again.

"You want to stop for a beer?" asked Angela after a few minutes. She never did stay mad long. Except for the day she threw me out.

"Where?" I asked. It was a dumb question. But I was wondering what she had in mind.

"How about the Oak Leaf? It's never crowded on a Wednesday night."

"Wednesday? Are you saying today is Wednesday?"

"Yeah, it's Wednesday. It's been Wednesday all day. What universe have you been living in?"

"I've been working seven days a week,

fifteen hours a day for weeks. You lose track of what day it is. But we had to get the crops in before the cold weather set in. There's nothing left now but a few pumpkins. They didn't need me for that."

"I guess," said Angela. She grinned suddenly. "Us city girls don't usually think about stuff like that. But what's so important about Wednesday?"

"It's Cheryl's day off. Remember? Ever since I first met her. She always took Wednesdays off."

"So?"

"Whoever set fire to the house wanted her dead too."

"Maybe. If he knew she was there."

"Lots of people did. She was always home asleep on Wednesday afternoons. Catching-up time, she called it."

"Could be," said Angela. "So how about that beer?"

"I haven't had a beer since I last saw you," I said. "Or any other kind of booze.

I was always too tired to go out with the crew after work."

"No wonder you're so thin. We can go for coffee, if you want."

We decided to go for coffee.

"Have you eaten?" I asked. We were strolling along, looking for someplace quiet.

"No, have you?" asked Angela.

"No. I watched Susanna eat most of a large pizza. It killed my appetite. Now I'm starving."

"Come on," said Angela. "How about a steak? My treat."

* * *

The steak house was almost empty. And very quiet. The waiter took our order and left us alone.

"Tell me," I said, "what have you heard about Freddie since I left?"

"Freddie who?"

"Come on, Angela. You know who I mean. My Freddie. The one who got me into this mess. The Freddie who swore in court that he had bribed me to suppress evidence. Dealer in drugs, women and anything else. If you could make money from it, Freddie was mixed up in it."

"Ah," she said. "That Freddie."

"I think maybe he was the body in my apartment," I said. "So I'm interested."

"I can understand that." She stopped to think.

I stood up. "Take your time," I said. "I'm off to the men's room."

"Sure," said Angela. "Go right ahead."

When I came back, she was putting her cell phone into her shirt pocket. I raised an eyebrow. She laughed.

"You still do that. It's easier to ask, you know. I was talking to my boss."

"At nine o'clock at night?"

"Sure. I have a new job. Didn't I tell you? The pay is good, but they want me to carry my mobile around all the time. That way, someone can call me at four in the morning. But they hardly ever use it."

The waiter put a platter of Italian-style antipasto and two plates down on the table.

"What did he want?" I asked, helping myself.

"Would I be on call for tomorrow's late shift. No big deal. Anyway, Freddie was sentenced in May," said Angela. "Just after you left for the farm."

"And?"

"He'd cut a deal—but you knew that—and told them everything they wanted to hear. So he got six months once they deducted time served. He was out in less than five, I think."

"So he just got out," I said. "But Freddie's small-time. He had nothing to do with those drug deals he confessed to."

"Why confess to them then?"

"Money. Rodriguez wanted to get rid of me. I was getting too close to him. So they paid him to frame me. By saying we were in it together."

"Are you sure? Or are you seeing conspiracies everywhere these days?"

"I'm sure," I said.

"So why burn down the house with him in it?" asked Angela. "What's the point? Wouldn't Rodriguez want him to be a witness in your trial?"

"That's what bothers me," I said. "It doesn't make sense."

"Can I treat you to a glass of wine with your dinner?" she said.

"No. I have to stay awake. I'm going back to the house tonight."

"Why?"

"Don't you think I have to see what's happening, Angela?"

"A waste of time, I would think," said Angela. "Tony said they were stopping for the night soon. He was anyway. Rachel's going to kill him if he doesn't come home. She invited two couples over for dinner."

"You'd think she would have learned by now," I said.

"He'll never be home every night at six," said Angela. "You never were. Of course, neither was I."

"And you'd think she'd get tired of yelling at him." I leaned forward. "Listen carefully, Angela," I whispered. "I think I can I hear her now."

We both burst out laughing. Rachel's temper was one of our old jokes.

"But it doesn't matter if he isn't there. I'm going anyway. I have a feeling it might be a good idea."

"You always were crazy," said Angela. "But if you want to sit there in the dark, go ahead. Just don't forget that you still have stuff at the apartment. You should come by and pick it up."

"What did I leave behind?"

"Just stuff."

"I'll call you later. Tomorrow for sure."

"Do that. Here come our steaks. I hope you can squeeze in a few minutes to eat yours."

"You don't have to be like that, Angela. I'll make time. I'm starving."

CHAPTER NINE

GREG

I went back to the park. This time I was sitting on the bench, relaxed and comfortable. There were only a couple of cops in uniform left at the scene. But the CSI team was there. And I recognized a couple of guys from the fire marshal's office. They were still working too. They don't like arson. No one seemed to notice me this time.

Then I saw someone walking over the wet grass toward me. I straightened up. He looked familiar. He was the man who had been talking to Angela.

"Terrible fire," he said, pausing to look

across the street. "I'm surprised there aren't more people out here."

"Maybe it's too cold and damp for them," I said.

"No. Usually with a big fire, you'll get a whole crowd standing around up to their knees in snow," he said. "Even at four in the morning."

"I guess. The morbid fascination of fire scenes."

"That's it. Do you mind if I sit down?"

"Go ahead. Do you like watching fires? Is that why you're here?" I asked.

"No. I knew the woman who died," he said. "Her name was Cheryl. She was a genuinely nice person."

"Really?"

He turned and looked at me.

"I know that sounds weak, but I don't say it about many people. I'll miss her."

We sat there, saying nothing.

"We have company," he said. "This is turning into a popular spot."

I turned to look. A big guy was crossing the street toward us. He was clearly visible in the bright lights. He looked neat and clean-cut. Like a model for men's work clothes. He stopped beside our bench and stared at the ruined house. "What's going on?" he asked. He shrugged a backpack off his shoulder and set it on the ground.

"There was a fire," I said.

"Well, yeah. I can see that. Why are you guys sitting here? Are you waiting for something to happen?"

"No," I said. "Just getting some fresh air."

"What about you? What are you doing?" asked the man sitting next to me.

"Hanging around," said the newcomer. "Waiting for my date. She won't be ready yet. I got off work early tonight."

"You work late?" I said.

"Sometimes. I'm an electrician, so I get called out when there's trouble."

"And there was trouble tonight?"

"Sort of. Whose house?"

"Mine," I said. "At least, I had an apartment in it."

"Jesus!" he said. "You must be upset. Did you lose much?"

"It was just a small apartment. There wasn't much in it."

The man sitting beside me stood up. "I'll leave you two here to watch over the house. There's not much I can do for Cheryl now." He turned to me. "If you rented her apartment, you must be Rick."

"That's me," I said.

"I'm Mark," he said. "Mark Davies." He reached out and shook my hand. "She used to talk about you."

The other stranger moved closer. "I'm Greg," he said. "Greg Hill. I'd better get going too."

They walked together through the wet leaves. At the sidewalk, they paused and said something to each other. Then Greg walked south. Mark walked north.

They both disappeared into the dark night. I sat where I was, thinking.

* * *

The CSI team was finally packing up. They put the last of the plastic bags filled with samples into boxes. They stacked the boxes carefully in their van. Then they went back over the ground again, checking. When that was done, they spread large sheets of heavy plastic over most of the ruin. One by one, the floodlights were turned off. The CSI team left one light burning, got in their van and drove away.

CHAPTER TEN

ATTACK

I was alone in the park, staring at the wreck of my apartment. There was an empty police car parked on the street. The two cops who had been left to guard the scene were leaning against it, talking quietly. The crime scene was deserted.

I sat on that bench and thought about Freddie. There were still people around. A car drove by. Two women walking together hurried down the street. They stopped to look at the house and then started off again. For a while I could hear their footsteps. They got fainter and fainter; then they stopped. A door slammed in the distance.

The night was deadly quiet. I returned to my thoughts. I was trying to figure out why someone would murder Cheryl and Freddie both. It wasn't hard to figure out why someone would murder Freddie. But Cheryl? I tried to see the link between them. It wasn't easy.

Then suddenly I couldn't see at all.

* * *

I blinked, panic-stricken. The whole world had gone black. But I could still hear. There was a screech of brakes. I turned. Two bright lights were shining in my eyes. A car. It seemed to have stopped in a panic. Then it started up again and came down the street, moving slowly.

That was a relief. I hadn't lost my sight. But all the houses were dark and the street-lights had gone out. The car's headlights lit up the two cops who had been left behind. One of them opened the door to the patrol car. The interior light went on. I could hear him talking. Calling in a report on the power failure, probably. The car kept going down the street, paying no attention to anyone or anything.

I looked around. The glow of city lights lit up the clouds a few blocks away in every direction. So the power had gone out just around here.

I decided to take advantage of the temporary darkness. I slipped across the road to the house. I figured I probably had at least fifteen minutes before a crew turned up and fixed the problem. I could do a lot of searching in fifteen minutes. I took out my flashlight. I could get into the basement a lot faster if I had some light. But then I thought about those two guys who had turned up in the park. And the two cops on the street.

I changed my mind. I went by feel instead, depending on my memory of the shape of the ruined building. I made my way over to the kitchen window in the back. It was broken. Reaching out cautiously,

I found jagged pieces of glass still in the frame. I took them out, one by one. As soon as I had enough space, I reached in to open the latch. And stopped. I heard a tiny click. Then a faint scraping sound. Something was moving around nearby. Very quietly. A night-prowling animal? I drew my hand out of the treacherous window frame. And listened. Another faint sound of movement.

I froze. Then something heavy cracked a piece of glass beside me. It seemed as loud as a pistol shot. I pulled my knees up to my belly and kicked out in the direction of the noise. I made contact. Someone swore.

I felt a sharp, brutal pain on the side of my head. Nothing more.

CHAPTER ELEVEN

NEW DIRECTIONS

I came swimming up to consciousness, feeling sick and dizzy. With a funny taste in my mouth. I lay very still, listening. Nothing moved. The world around me was calm and peaceful. Except that someone had whacked me on the head. I rolled over onto my hands and knees, feeling for my flashlight. It was gone. I pushed myself to my feet and kicked over a pile of broken glass.

"You in there," yelled someone. "Stop where you are. Come out with your hands above your head."

I wondered how I was supposed to do that.

"Or we're coming in to get you," he added.

"Hey, Jeff," said another voice. "He's over here. The other side of the street."

I heard the sound of heavy footsteps running and another shout of "Stop where you are!" I straightened up, more cautiously this time. I leaned against the wrecked back wall of the house. A piece of rubble slithered over another piece of rubble. The wall began weaving back and forth.

No. The wall wasn't moving. I was. I waited until the world went back to normal. Then I took a step. Okay. I moved over to the driveway. Very carefully. I walked back to the garage. There the darkness was total. Something ran past my foot. A rat? Or a cat? A cat or a rat. The words repeated themselves over and over in my head. *Cat, rat. Rat, cat.* "Stop that," I said.

I couldn't tell if I said it out loud. The thought that I might have scared me enough to get me moving again. Leaning on the garage with one hand, I managed to reach the back fence. I went out the gate and into the alleyway. I moved to the other side and felt my way along. These alleys were lined with high fences. Most of them had gates that were kept locked at night.

The glow in the night sky seemed even brighter here. The power must be on nearby, I figured. But I was trapped in this alley, deep in the shadows. And feeling sick and dizzy. I had to get out. The closest exit that I could remember was at the back of a convenience store. There was a walkway running beside it. It led through to the next street.

It seemed a mile away. I felt my way along the fence until I came to a gap. I turned and headed for the light. The power failure ended in the middle of the street in front of me. The other side of the street had lights, music blaring and flickering television screens. I blinked and headed north. Toward noise and traffic and people.

At West Central Avenue I turned right without thinking. I walked past restaurants and shops. Past a little park with a statue of someone in it. No one knew who he was. Or why he was there. Maybe he used to be important. At the corner was a four-story apartment building. I looked up. There were lights on in the top-floor corner apartment. I walked up to the front door and tried to open it. It was locked. I reached into my pocket for my keys. Then I remembered I didn't have keys to the apartment anymore.

"Rick! Great to see you. Welcome home." The voice was loud and cheerful. It belonged to the male half of the couple who lived on the third floor. They were leaning on each other. He grinned at me. She giggled.

"Hi," I said. "Was it a good party?"

"Great!" They unlocked the door and held it open for me. It was a safe question. They were always coming back from a party. I smiled.

"Thanks. It's nice to be back," I muttered and held the elevator door open for them.

So much for thinking that no one could recognize me.

* * *

When the door opened, I walked into the apartment like I still lived there.

"Rick," said Angela. "What in hell are you doing here?"

"I'm not sure," I said. "I got caught in the blackout."

"What are you talking about? Come into the living room and sit down like a civilized human being," she said.

I walked into the living room. Tony was sprawled on the big armchair. My big armchair. Across from him was Mark. The guy from the park. My stomach twisted in a spasm of pure rage and jealousy.

CHAPTER TWELVE

THE APARTMENT

I couldn't believe what I was seeing.

"What are you doing here?" I asked the guy from the park.

"Angela and I are old friends," said Mark.

I'd never heard of him. That made this little get-together seem even more awkward.

"What happened to you?" he asked.

"Nothing," I snapped.

"You're dripping blood."

"My god," said Angela. "What happened?"

"Nothing." I reached up and touched the side of my head. It was wet. I looked at my hand. There was blood on it.

"Sorry," I said, staring at the blood. "The power went out. I walked into something in the dark and hit my head. Stupid of me. But I'm fine." I was talking too much. I knew it but I couldn't stop.

"Sit down," said Angela, pushing me onto the couch. "Can you give me hand, Mark?"

They headed for the kitchen. Tony came over and sat down beside me.

"Why in hell did you come back?" he asked.

"I wanted to find out what was going on," I said.

"Nothing until today."

"Did I tell you I got a message from Rodriguez?" I whispered.

"Rodriguez? What did he want?"

"Hard to tell. Anyway, it wasn't exactly from him. It was from one of his guys. But it sounded like having the current investigations into his activities dropped was worth a million or two to him."

"And what did you tell him?"

"I told his little friend he was talking to the wrong guy."

"Look, Rick, we have to talk. Seriously. Tomorrow." He stood up and went back to the armchair. Angela and Mark came in with a stack of towels, a first-aid kit and a basin filled with water. I tried to get up.

"Sit still," said Angela crossly.

I sat still. She mopped up the blood and slapped a square dressing on the side of my head.

"Does your head hurt?" she asked.

"Yes," I admitted.

"Mark, get me some ice from the freezer, will you? Put it in a plastic bag."

"Right away, captain," he said.

"Look straight at me, Rick."

I did.

"You look wonderful, baby," I said. "And I feel like hell."

She stared into my eyes.

"I don't think you have a concussion.

But what happened?" she asked again. "Who hit you?"

"The lights went out over by the house and I walked into something in the dark."

"Yeah, sure," said Angela. "You said that already. I didn't believe it the first time either."

The last thing I heard was Angela saying, "You guys better go. I'll keep an eye on him. I'll see you in the morning, Mark."

When I woke up again I was lying on the couch, covered with a duvet. Someone had stripped me down to my underwear. There was a pillow under my head.

The sun was pouring in the window. My watch was sitting on the coffee table by the couch. It was almost nine o'clock. There was a note on the table.

Hi. I'm at work. Help yourself to coffee and anything else you can find in the kitchen. There are plenty of clean towels in the cupboard. I'll pick you up here at 11:00. We have to be at headquarters at 11:30 to be interviewed. See you then. Angela.

It wasn't exactly affectionate. But it wasn't dripping hate either. I got up cautiously and headed for the shower.

After a shower, coffee, toast and juice, I was feeling reasonably okay again. I tidied up the mess I made in the kitchen and took more coffee into the living room. I grabbed a pad of paper and a pencil from Angela's desk. I looked at it for a while, and then I put down a word or two for everything that had happened yesterday. *Man in basement. Fire. Susanna.* And so on. I ended up with fifteen or twenty of them.

After studying them, I took out a pencil and drew lines connecting them. I erased some of the lines and connected them up in different ways. In the end I had a small web of possible connections. And a few glimmers of an idea.

It was time to get to work again.

CHAPTER THIRTEEN

SPINNING THE WEB

I checked my little address book. I found Luke's name. He was a kid who had worked with me for a while. That was a couple of years ago. He was clear-headed, hard-working and careful. And I had recommended him for promotion. I phoned him. It was time to call in a few favors.

I made two more phone calls after that. The first took a long time. At last my contact came up with some answers. I jotted them down on my chart. A picture was emerging. The last call was brief. It was in Spanish.

"Hi, Paco," I said. "Ricardo Montoya. I need to contact Rodriguez."

The answer wasn't encouraging.

"What's he doing in Mexico?" I asked.

"Christmas is coming, Ricardo. He's gone to see his family."

"It's still October, Paco," I said. "Look, I have to talk to him. Can I phone him? Will he phone me?"

"Send him an email," said Paco. He gave me an address. "That's what I do. Just remember that someone is probably reading his mail. Don't confess to any crimes."

Judging by the howls of laughter, he thought that was pretty funny.

"Thanks, Paco," I said. "I'll remember that."

I sent it from Angela's computer. She still hadn't changed her password. It was just a brief note in Spanish. *Rodriguez. Did you know Freddie Hancock died in a fire yesterday? Who lit the match? Ricardo Montoya.*

The answer came back before Angela returned to pick me up. *Ricardo. It must have been you. Thanks and well done. And if it wasn't you, someone else is trying to slit your throat. Not me. Why burn down the barn just to kill a rat? R.*

It was depressing. Even the crooks figured I had wiped out Freddie.

* * *

Angela turned up before eleven. She was carrying a garment bag over her arm. She came sweeping into the room like a brisk wind.

"Here," she said. "Clean clothes."

"Where did you get them?"

"At your hotel."

"How did you do that?" I asked.

"It was easy. I flashed my ID, your room key and a note from you giving me permission. No problem."

"I don't remember giving you a note..."

"You don't? That's funny. I thought you had. If you'd rather go downtown in blood-stained clothes and muddy jeans, okay. I'll take them back."

"Dammit, Angela. Of course I wouldn't. Anyway, thanks."

I came out of the bathroom in clean clothes, looking respectable. For the first time I really noticed the apartment.

"It looks just the same," I said. "Only not as messy."

"You know why that is," she said.

"I've changed," I said. "Honest, I have. For five months I've been living in a small room with three other guys. I've learned to be neat. I can't believe how big the apartment looks. It's amazing."

"The owner wants to sell off the two top floors as condos," she said. "I'm considering buying this place, if he doesn't want too much money for it."

I started prowling through it, thinking of what I had thrown away.

"Come on," she said. "Let's get going."

* * *

As soon as we walked into the stationhouse, we saw Susanna.

"Poor Susanna," said Angela. "This must be tough for her. Who's the big guy with her?"

"That's interesting," I said. "It's Greg. The guy in the park who was waiting for his date."

"Maybe the date was Susanna. That's very interesting."

"Yes. It would explain why he's here."

Susanna turned and saw us. "Do you know where we're supposed to go?" she asked.

"The last room on your right," said Angela, pointing.

They headed off like a pair of greyhounds at the track. We followed them. Slowly. Two men ushered us in and stood beside the door. To keep us there, I guess.

I recognized the room as soon as we walked into it. Green and brown paint. A long table at one end. Ten or twelve battered desks lined up facing the table. I spent a lot of time in it when I first started. At training sessions. And endless meetings.

Luke was sitting behind the table. Beside him was one of the guys from the Crime Scene Investigation unit. The third man was a sergeant from another division. He looked familiar. Luke was resting his hand on a stack of papers. Tony, Susanna, and Greg were already sitting at the desks. We joined them.

The sergeant looked at us and checked a sheet in front of him. "We appreciate you coming in, since you're all witnesses in this case. Except for Mr. Greg Hill, who is here as a friend of Susanna Vicars."

"She asked me to come in with her," said Greg. "She's upset because of her mother's death."

"Very understandable," said the sergeant. "And I'm sure she has our deepest sympathy."

Luke handed him a thin folder. The
sergeant opened it and glanced over the
material in front of him.

"Good," he said briskly. "Each of you
can cast light on yesterday's tragic events.
The fire. The death of Cheryl Vicars and of
an unknown person."

Luke handed him a sheet of paper.

"That person has been tentatively identified as Freddie Hancock."

Everyone nodded but Susanna. But I
don't suppose the sergeant expected her to.

"You are all here voluntarily to make a
statement. Once you have signed your statement, you should be free to leave."

Should be free to leave? I would have
been happier if he had said, "You *will* be
free to leave." I looked over at the uniforms
standing at the door. I wondered if anyone
else noticed what he had just said.

CHAPTER FOURTEEN

COLLATERAL DAMAGE

Now I remembered that smooth, gentle voice. Sergeant Frank Donovan. I used to watch him lay traps with that kind voice and gentle manner. His sympathetic smile suckered people into saying just what he wanted. I had learned a lot from him in my early days on the force. Then he was promoted, and I lost track of him. I thought he had retired long ago.

"Sergeant Montoya," he said. "When the fire broke out, you were at your lawyer's office, I believe. Is that so?"

The door squeaked open. Mark Davies slipped in and sat on the other side of Angela.

I waited until he was settled.

"I don't know, sir," I said. "When did the fire break out?"

"When were you at your lawyer's office?" asked Donovan.

"I had an appointment for two o'clock. I got there about ten minutes early."

"Did anyone see you at ten minutes to two?"

I thought for a moment.

"Three people. My lawyer's partner and a law student who works there were in the reception area talking to Amanda. She's the receptionist. Maybe five minutes after that, a courier came in with a package."

"Thank you. And now, Sergeant Marchetti?"

Tony explained that he was on his lunch hour, eating across the street from 52 Division.

"Thank you. Ms. Vicars?" And we went through the others, Susanna having her hair done, Angela and Mark at work. "And you, Mr. Hill?" he asked.

Greg looked up, a little bit shocked.

"I was at work. It should have been my afternoon off, but I was called out. But it shouldn't matter, because I'm not really a witness, am I? Just a friend of Susanna."

"Of course," said Sergeant Donovan and reached out his hand. Luke put another folder in it. We sat there staring at him as he read through it. He looked up.

"The fire. We need to establish the cause of the fire. We're hoping you might be able to give us some useful background information."

"What do you mean?" asked Susanna.

"Was Mrs. Vicars a careless, easygoing sort of woman? Did she smoke?"

"Neither one," said Mark quickly. "A non-smoker and a worrier."

"Could you explain that, Mr. Davies?"

"She recently installed smoke detectors on every floor, fire extinguishers in all three kitchens, and put in a fire escape from the second and third floors."

"How do you know?" I asked.

"We were friends. She asked my advice. I recommended the firm that installed the safety equipment. Then I inspected the house after it was done. I can assure you that everything was installed properly."

"Is this an area you specialize in, Mr. Davies?" asked Sergeant Donovan.

"It is."

Donovan wrote something on the folder in front of him and handed it back to Luke. Luke passed another folder to the sergeant.

"And now we come to the identity of the man in the basement," said Donovan. "He has been tentatively identified as Fred Hancock. At the time of his death, he appeared to be living in Sergeant Montoya's apartment. What can you tell us about him, Sergeant Montoya? Was he renting the apartment from you? Or was he a friend you were helping out?"

"Neither one, sir," I said. "But I had run into him in the course of my work. He did not have my permission to be in my apartment."

"Who was paying the rent?" asked the guy from CSI.

"I had paid the rent until the end of December," I said, trying to remember where I had put the receipt that Cheryl had given me.

"How long had he been living in the apartment?" asked Donovan, looking around.

"I don't know, sir," I said. Long enough to pile up a sinkful of dishes. But I wasn't going to bring that up.

"I would say that he arrived sometime after Friday morning," said Mark Davies. "Mrs. Vicars did not mention him on Friday. On Tuesday she was disturbed about a stranger living in the basement. Apparently he had changed the lock on the apartment."

"You spoke to her on Tuesday?" Mark nodded. "Had she invited the stranger in?"

"I don't know," said Mark. "She was a private sort of person."

"Sergeant Montoya, did you know Mr. Hancock?" asked Donovan.

Everyone in the room knew that I had known him. Except, maybe, Greg.

I nodded. "He had been involved in an investigation that I was working on."

"When you say involved, what do you mean?" asked Donovan.

"He was an informant. He was prepared to testify against a person of interest to us. This person could have been charged with serious offenses," I said carefully.

"So it is possible that the fire was started to dispose of Mr. Hancock, and that Mrs. Vicars's death was an unfortunate coincidence. 'Collateral Damage' as they call it."

"It is certainly possible, sir."

CHAPTER FIFTEEN

TONY

Sergeant Donovan left. We all spread out a bit and made statements. They were read, checked and signed.

Susanna and Greg grabbed their coats and left without a word to anyone.

I turned to Angela. "How about lunch?"

"Sorry," she said, "I have to get back to work." She opened her wallet and pulled out a card. "Your room key," she added. "I borrowed it. Call me tonight."

I watched her walk out with Mark Davies, laughing about something.

"Tough luck," said a voice behind me. A familiar voice.

"Hi, Tony," I said.

"Quit worrying about Angela and let's get some lunch. We have a lot of stuff to talk about."

"Good idea," I said.

"She quit, you know," said Tony. "Right after you left town. She was upset. And a couple of the guys were making bad jokes about you being in trouble. She blew up and walked out."

"She has a temper," I said. "Let's go."

* * *

Tony's favorite Italian restaurant was crowded. But the owner found us a table. They like him there.

"How's Susanna?" asked Tony. "I wanted to talk to her too. But she took off like a scared rabbit with that overgrown kid, Greg. Is she okay?"

"I don't know," I said. "I saw her yesterday, right after the fire. She looked to be in shock, shivering with cold. So I took her for a pizza."

"I'm not surprised."

"But the weird thing is that she looked amazing. She had a gorgeous red dress on. Hair and makeup like a model. You must have seen her. Didn't you notice?"

"Yesterday?" I nodded. "No. No red dress. I think I saw her in her usual jeans and black sweater. Neat, clean jeans and sweater."

"I guess she changed at work."

"Probably. Look, Rick—that stuff you said last night about Rodriguez was all bullshit, wasn't it?"

"Yeah, it was. I was sort of out of it. It seemed a good idea at the time. I wanted to see how you'd react. But, of course, you didn't."

"You should know by now that I don't fall into your traps." He grinned. "But I want to know what made you come back? Just in time for Freddie to get incinerated?"

"Believe it or not, it was because my job was over. I picked up my pay and came down to the terminal with the last load of apples. End of season."

"Nothing to do with Freddie?"

"Everything to do with Freddie. Except for the date. But I was not expecting him to be in my apartment. And I was certainly not planning on him being dead. I wanted to talk to him."

"And did you?"

"No. I got to the apartment. I saw that someone was living there. I had no idea it was Freddie. But I was mad as hell. It was around six, I guess. I'd been up and working since four in the morning. I needed to shower and change. I figured it could wait. I got a room, went to bed and slept for twelve hours."

"Did you go down to the house then?"

"No, I spent the morning getting cleaned up and buying some clothes that fit me. Then I went to see the lawyer. I saw some-thing on the news about the fire and went down to see what had happened. I figured that Cheryl and Susanna were at work."

"But it was Wednesday."

"I know you won't believe me, Tony, but I lost track of the days up there."

"I don't believe you."

"I was working seven days a week from before dawn to after dusk. Doing the same thing, over and over again. The days blend into each other. It sounds feeble. But it's the truth."

The waitress set down two bowls of pasta. As soon as she left, Tony leaned forward.

"So who's on your short list of guys with torches? Besides me, of course."

"You?" I said.

"Of course. We're at the top of everybody's list. We're the guys Rodriguez would try to bribe."

"Makes sense," I said carefully.

"So if it was Rodriguez, he was aiming to get rid of Freddie and one of us."

"Kill Freddie and put the blame on me, more likely. He'd already set me up with that money stuffed under my mattress."

"The problem's going to be getting to Rodriguez," said Tony.

"He's left town," I said.

"I heard that. Where is he?"

"Mexico. For Christmas." I raised my hand. "Don't say it. It's still October. But that's what I was told."

"That's not going to be easy."

"Not that hard. I sent him an email. I asked him who torched Freddie. He answered."

"No shit. He answered?"

I took the printout from my pocket and handed it over.

"It's in Spanish."

"Well, of course it is. But he says two things. He isn't the one trying to cut my throat, and he wouldn't burn down a barn to kill a rat. It's just possible he had nothing to do with it."

"Maybe. Who else then?"

"Who could get in the house?" I asked.

"Without breaking in? The two of us."

"And four other people, I think. Susanna, Angela's friend Mark, Angela…"

"And Susanna's friend, Greg," said Tony. "And since Freddie was living there, any one of Rodriguez's guys."

"Let's start with Angela. I refuse to believe that Angela would set fire to Cheryl's house."

"Where is she working now?" asked Tony.

"I don't know. Do you?"

"I haven't heard. She hasn't exactly been on good terms with our side lately," he said. "Although she did go down to the morgue and tell me the body wasn't you."

"She was probably disappointed," I said bitterly.

He shook his head.

"No, Rick. Actually she sounded worried. But something else is bothering me."

"What's that?"

"Mark Davies. He said that Cheryl had installed alarms and fire extinguishers. So why didn't she hear the smoke alarm?"

asked Tony. "They told me she didn't even try to get up. It doesn't make sense."

"I wonder," I said. "And I want to know when Susanna changed her clothes. Did she bring all that stuff with her to work? Are her jeans and sweater still there?"

"I'd like to find out something about Greg," said Tony.

"And who in hell is Mark?" I said.

CHAPTER SIXTEEN

THE WEB

I refused the offer of a ride from Tony. It was at least three miles to my hotel, but I walked. I needed to move around. I had to clear my head.

Meanwhile, a small group of cops at the station had started asking questions. When did Susanna change from her jeans into her red dress? What was Mark's background? What was his connection with Cheryl? Who was Greg? And in the lab, technicians were busy analyzing the samples from the site of the fire. They had already finished writing some early reports on their findings.

* * *

My hotel room wasn't any more inviting than it had been the day before. I sat on the bed. I turned on the TV and watched it for five minutes. I turned it off again. I went down-stairs and bought a paper. There were a few pictures of the fire, mostly of the house. And there was a lot of written coverage as well. But there was nothing really new. A lot of descriptions of Cheryl and Susanna from people who didn't know them. Most of it was garbage.

I shoved the paper in the basket.

* * *

At seven I called Angela.

"You said I should come over and pick up my stuff," I said.

She admitted that she had said that.

"Come on over."

The apartment smelled warm and inviting. I hung up my jacket and looked around. I had expected to find a pile of my things by the entrance door. There was nothing there.

"Where's my stuff?" I said. "In the junk room?"

I opened the door to the second bedroom. That was where we used to throw everything we didn't have a place for. I turned on the overhead light. I stepped back, amazed. All the junk was gone. Angela had stripped off the hideous wallpaper and replaced it with a soft yellow paint. She had hung new curtains on the windows.

"You've fixed it up," I said.

"You noticed."

"Are you planning to rent it out?"

"Of course not," she said impatiently. "I just decided to do it. And I did."

"Okay, okay, don't get mad," I said. I didn't feel like fighting. "But what did I leave behind?"

"Not much. A couple of pictures. Some photographs. A whole lot of hurt feelings. Even more memories. Not much that you can carry away."

"God, Angela, I'm so sorry," I said. I reached out to take her hands.

She backed away. As if she couldn't bear to be close to me.

"You can't believe how sorry I am," I said. "For being so stupid. And stubborn."

"And drunk," she added. "Don't forget that. Come on. Let's get out of here. It still smells of paint and disappointment."

I followed her into the living room.

"I called and left a message at your apartment," she said. "Like you told me to if I had to get in touch. You never called me back."

"I collected my messages at least once a week," I said. "I never heard from you. Was it important?"

"It was important when I called. It doesn't matter now." She sounded bitter and unhappy.

"What was it?" I said. "You've got to tell me what it was, Angela."

"I don't have to tell you anything," she said. "But I didn't ask you over so we could fight. I'm cooking supper. I'd appreciate it if you'd join me. Today wasn't much fun, was it?"

"You want me to stay for supper?"

"That's what I said. I'd rather not be alone for now."

"Sure," I said. I would have agreed to anything right then. Besides, I suddenly felt hungry. "What can I do?"

"Throw a salad together. As soon as the water boils I'll put on the noodles."

"What are we having?"

"Baked chicken and mushrooms."

And so we worked together in the kitchen, side by side, the way we used to. When things were better. "No red onions?" I said, my head in the refrigerator.

"If you'd wanted red onions you should have bought some."

"How was I supposed to know? Hey— where did you get these olives? Nice work."

I put the salad bowl on the table, cut some chunks of bread and drained the pasta. Angela tasted the sauce from the chicken.

"How is it?" I asked.

"Good. I tried some fresh rosemary in it. It works."

And we sat down to eat, talking food. I told her about cooking on a tiny budget with the crew on the farm.

"I picked up a lot of new ideas," I said. "The guys in the crew always send as much money home as they can, so we bought as little as possible. Tiny pieces of meat, oil, flour, salt, hot pepper sauce. Otherwise we lived on fruit and vegetables."

"No parties?"

"Never. On Saturday nights the crew went into town for a beer. One beer."

"And you didn't go?" She didn't sound as if she believed me.

"I didn't go."

We were cleaning up the kitchen. I was beginning to wonder about possibilities for the rest of the evening. Then Angela's mobile buzzed unpleasantly. She plucked it out of the little leather holder fastened to her belt and flipped it open.

"Damn," she muttered. "Hi. What's going on?" She paused. "Right. See you there. Fifteen minutes."

"Sorry, Rick," she said. "My boss. I've been called out. Something's up."

"What in hell do you do?" I asked.

"I'm still a cop, sort of. Private security and investigative stuff. It's interesting, but it does have a few drawbacks. Like getting calls on my evenings off. But this is a case I'm on, so it's my baby."

All the time she was talking, she was getting ready to go out. "I'll drop you at your hotel," she said. "Maybe we can get together tomorrow."

It suddenly occurred to me that we hadn't once talked about the fire.

CHAPTER SEVENTEEN

THE FOURTH DAY

My mobile buzzed frantically. It was midmorning. I was outside, walking aimlessly along West Central. It was Tony.

"We have to talk."

"Okay. Where are you?"

"At the Coffee Corner. You walked by me three minutes ago. I waved, but you didn't see me."

I was back at the Coffee Corner in two minutes. I nodded at the waitress. A nice kid, but she wasn't Cheryl.

"Coffee?" she asked.

"Sure." Between breakfast and lunch, the place was almost empty. She looked bored.

Tony walked over to the big round table in the corner and sat down.

"Are you expecting a crowd?" I asked.

"A couple more people," said Tony. "I have some interesting results I wanted to talk about. They weren't easy to get."

"Why?"

"It's like this, Rick. I've actually been off your case since Monday. The guys upstairs decided I was a bit too close to you."

"But that was always true."

He shrugged his shoulders. "Then yesterday morning they decided to put me on leave. Except that I had to turn up for Donovan's little inquiry. So I'm on leave."

"Why aren't you home sleeping?"

"Too boring. I thought I'd see if I could find out what was going on."

"Did you?"

"I'm getting there. Have you come up with anything I should know, Rick? Before the others get here."

"Like what?"

"What has Angela told you? I haven't been able to talk to her."

"Nothing. And that's because Angela had nothing to do with Freddie. He was my problem. Or with Cheryl's death or the fire."

"How can you be sure? She's being pretty cagey, isn't she?"

"Listen, if she had anything to do with Cheryl's death, Tony, I'm finished. I'd have nothing left I could trust. Or believe in. Anyway, she was never involved in the mess with Rodriguez."

"Really?" He looked at me, his head tilted. "Did you ask her? Do anything to check her out?"

"No!"

"I don't believe you."

"That's not my fault."

"Sorry, Rick. God, I hate not working," he said. "It makes me crazy."

At that moment, a small white van pulled up outside the Coffee Corner. Susanna and Greg had arrived.

"Hi, Tony," said Susanna. "We made it. You not working today?"

"I'm off," said Tony.

"Again?" she said. "You were off on Wednesday too, weren't you? Or so they said." She winked. She was needling him, and he was reacting.

"No, Susanna. I wasn't off on Wednesday. Anyway, I don't work seven days a week. None of us do."

"I at least have a reason to be off. I get three days for the death of a mother," she said. "It's in our contract."

"I know what's in the contract," said Tony.

"Lay off, Susanna," I said before they started yelling at each other. "Sit down. Coffee?"

Greg paid no attention. He was staring out the window. "I hope I don't get a ticket," he said. "I have this sign on the dash: *On Call. Emergency Service.* But they never pay any attention to it."

"Sit still," said Tony. "If you get a ticket, I'll pay it. I promise."

The door opened again and Angela came in, followed by Mark Davies.

The meeting had come to order.

* * *

"So what are we doing here?" asked Susanna.

"It was my idea," said Tony. "I'm not on this case. I'm just a possible witness, like the rest of you. And like Rick, my name has been associated with Fred Hancock."

"I think Tony's trying to say that we all have an interest in finding out what happened on Wednesday," I said.

"Thanks, Rick," said Tony. "They'd never have figured it out on their own, would they?"

"Calm down, Tony, and tell us what you've been able to find out."

"How?" asked Susanna.

"I have friends, Susanna," he said. "So this is real stuff. First of all, some of the data from the burn site has come in."

"Like what?" asked Greg.

"It was Freddie who died in the basement," said Tony.

"How can they be sure?" asked Susanna.

"He's been booked often enough. So his prints are on file. They got enough bits of skin from his fingertips to get a match."

Susanna looked as if she wished she hadn't asked.

"And they've confirmed the cause of the fire."

"What was it?" I asked.

"What you'd expect," said Tony. "Nothing fancy. Just rags soaked with lots of gasoline. Lots of traces of them in the basement and on the first floor."

Susanna and Greg shifted impatiently. Angela and Mark sat quietly, looking interested but not surprised. They could have been at a lecture on gardening or modern art.

"The third result was sort of a surprising," said Tony. "Although it does explain why your alarm system wasn't more helpful, Mr. Davies."

"What failed?" he asked. "I am upset that Cheryl died in a fire. I feel some responsibility. She was a very courageous woman, but she was afraid of fire. She took precautions against it. They didn't help."

"Nothing failed, Mr. Davies," said Tony. "Cheryl and Freddie had both taken—or been given—large doses of a narcotic substance. They were probably unconscious."

"See?" said Susanna. "Drugs. Rodriguez again. I'll bet Freddie and Cheryl were smoking something, or even injecting something, really powerful that this Rodriguez gave to Freddie."

"And then they spread gasoline all over the place and set fire to it? Just for fun? Come on, Susanna," I said, furious for the moment.

"I didn't mean that," she said. "Cheryl was in bed, wasn't she? And it must have been someone trying to get rid of Freddie who started the fire. Not knowing that anyone else was in the house. After all, how many people have Wednesdays off?"

"Or maybe whoever did it knew Cheryl took Wednesdays off," said Mark Davies suddenly.

CHAPTER EIGHTEEN

DEATH INSURANCE

"Who would want to kill my mother?" Susanna's face was white. "She never hurt a fly. Everyone loved her."

"That's true, Susanna. I did," said Mark in a low voice. "All of us did. It was a part of what she was. But she had another side. She was careful. She worried about the future. She saved her money and was well insured. House and life insurance."

"How do you know?" said Susanna. "Who is this guy?" she asked, looking around.

"Sources," he said. "So the beneficiary is going to do well."

"That's interesting," said Tony.

"But I'm the beneficiary, aren't I? Are you saying I killed my own mother? Me?" Her eyes filled with tears.

"Did she own the house?" asked Tony.

"She did," said Mark. "She paid the mortgage off last year."

"How do you know all this?" I asked.

"I knew her pretty well. I came here for breakfast. I sat over there, by the coffee machine. After the place emptied out, we used to talk. I don't suppose you and Angela even noticed me."

He turned to Susanna. "It doesn't have to have been you," he said. "Someone else might want you to be rich. Someone looking for a wife with money."

"Either way, that made Cheryl the target of the fire," said Tony.

"It's possible," said Mark. "Whenever you're talking about a lot of money, you have a motive. Money changes things."

"Yes," said Tony. "It changes things."

"I always figured the motive was money," I said. "But I still think Rodriguez was trying to get rid of Freddie. After all, he was going to talk. But Cheryl's death? I couldn't see it. Unless she was going to tell us why she let Freddie stay in my apartment."

"Weren't there easier ways to get rid of Freddie?" asked Angela.

"Torching the house brought me into the frame," I said. "And that meant someone wanted to fix me for good. That someone has to be Rodriguez."

"It looks that way," said Mark.

"So I started things rolling. I told a couple of people I was going to poke around the site of the fire."

"Who?" asked Mark.

"Angela and Susanna. Then I went over to see if anyone turned up."

"You bastard!" said Angela. "You suspected me?"

"Of course not," I said. "But I wanted to make sure. After all, you were pretty angry."

"I had reason to be," said Angela.

"I know. But..."

"Save the fights for later," said Mark. "What did they do?"

"Angela told me I was crazy," I said. "That made me feel better. Of course, I didn't feel so wonderful when I turned up at her apartment and saw you there, Mark. I didn't know you two knew each other."

"And Susanna?" asked Angela.

"Nothing much. I went over to the park and waited. Mark turned up. And then Greg. Interesting, I thought. You tell two women and two guys turn up."

"I told you," said Greg. "I was just killing time until I could go and pick up Susanna. When I called her, she said to give her thirty minutes to pull herself together, like. She'd meet me outside Jenny's house. Isn't that what you said, Susanna?"

"Something like that," said Susanna.

"Can we get away from the damn park for a minute?" asked Tony. "There's no law against sitting and talking to people in a public park at nine or ten at night."

"Look, Tony. Two things happened at the park that night that shouldn't have."

"What?"

"Someone screwed up the power lines. And someone hit me on the head. If his aim had been better, I'd be dead."

"Who?" said Angela.

"It's pretty obvious. Most of us wouldn't have the guts to play around with high tension wires. But there's an electrician in the room. Sitting right there. How's your leg, Greg? Weren't you limping just a little? How much damage did I do?"

All the eyes turned on Greg.

He pushed his chair back. "Okay. I went over to see what was happening. Just like you, Rick." He stood up. "I bumped into Rick in the dark. He fell and hit his head. I bruised my ankle. No big deal.

I apologize, Rick. Let's go home, Susanna."

"Wait a minute," said Susanna. "Forget Greg. He knew nothing about what was going on."

"Really? Who did then?" I asked.

"Tony. He used Greg. He needed help from someone with no connections to Rodriguez or the police."

"How do you know?" I asked.

"Greg told me," she said. "This morning. He asked me what to do."

Greg sat down, burying his head in his hands.

"Why would Tony do it?" I asked.

She looked around. Everyone in the room was staring at her. As if she was a snake coiled up on the table, ready to strike.

"For the money. I think he had big gambling debts."

"Tony?" said Angela. "He doesn't even play poker with the guys."

"Sure," said Susanna. "That's what everyone thinks."

"We don't just think it, Susanna. We know it," I said. "Anyway, Rachel would break his nose if he did."

"She would, Susanna," said Tony, grinning. "Believe me. And she knows every cent I spend."

"He's conning you, Rick. The way he's always conned everybody. I've been working around these guys for almost two years, and I can see it."

"See what?" asked Tony.

"Your connections with Rodriguez," said Susanna. "Even the soccer team he coaches. It's filled with kids who've been busted for dealing."

"Okay," I said, "let's say Tony did it. Why involve Greg?" I wondered what she'd say.

"He needed someone with a truck that no one would notice. Greg's truck was always around our place. So he asked Greg. They put the cans of gas and stuff in the truck. He drove it to our place and waited in the truck for Tony. When I found out about it, I knew Rodriguez was behind it. And was going to put the blame on you, Rick."

"So why did Greg try to kill me?"

"He told you! He wasn't trying to kill you. Don't you ever listen?" said Susanna.

CHAPTER NINETEEN

THE PRICE OF A LIFE

Susanna stood up. "Come on, Greg. We're leaving. These guys aren't working cops. They have no right to ask us questions. They're just playing games."

"Just a minute, Susanna," I said. "You're right, of course. But we can call in the real troops in a second when we want. Hang on. The party isn't over yet."

"Anyone looking at the evidence is going to assume you killed your mother, Susanna," said Angela. "Go ahead. Convince us you didn't."

"There's no point," said Tony. "She did it. Or, at least, she's responsible for Cheryl's death. We won't have any trouble proving it either."

Susanna sat there quietly. She seemed perfectly relaxed now.

"Why did you do it, Susanna?" I asked. "Cheryl was your mother."

"Greed," said Tony. "Rodriguez probably paid her a bundle. First to put Freddie in your apartment where they could find him. And then to get rid of him. We'll find the money. It's very hard stuff to hide."

"How much did you get to kill two people, Susanna?" I asked. "What's the price of a life right now?"

"You stupid bastards," she said. "I didn't touch Cheryl. But I won't pretend that I'm sorry she's dead. I hated her."

"Why?" I asked. Even then—even suspecting she killed Cheryl—I was stunned.

"Because Cheryl was rich. And we lived like beggars. Do you know what that's like?"

"Dead, she was rich," said Mark. "Not while she was alive."

"That's not true. My father left her lots of money. But she never spent anything.

She rented out most of the house. She worked as a waitress." Susanna's cheeks were red with anger. "She could have sent me to private school and bought us both nice clothes. We could have had a car. Instead, she made me get a job. And pay rent on my apartment."

"She put your father's insurance money aside for you, Susanna," said Mark. "It was for emergencies and to get you a good start in life."

She wasn't listening.

"It served her right, dying in the fire. But I had nothing to do with it. And you'll never be able to prove that I did."

"Everyone makes mistakes, Susanna," I said, "Even you. You know why they called me the Spider? I was after this rich, powerful guy with important friends. A real bastard."

Tony nodded. "Rick wove a huge web. And the bastard made one mistake. Rick caught him. One very big fly. So we called him the Spider."

"And this time I wove a very small web and caught a big fool and a nasty little fly," I said.

CHAPTER TWENTY

THE MISTAKE

Susanna stood up, slowly and deliberately. She nodded and walked out. Greg scrambled after her. Tony was already on his mobile, talking fast. What happened next came very quickly. Afterward, no one was really sure what order it all happened in. Angela said that Greg was the first to notice anything. She's probably right. She was the first of us to go outside after them.

There was hardly any traffic on West Central Avenue. Greg's truck was parked right at the curb in front of us. It was pointed east. He started walking around to the driver's side. A slow-moving westbound patrol car braked suddenly. It made a u-turn on the almost empty street. Greg stopped and walked back toward the sidewalk. Susanna started to run. Angela sprinted forward and grabbed Susanna's arm. Susanna screamed.

When I came out of the Coffee Corner, Greg was lunging at Angela. That was a mistake. She kicked him hard, where it hurt. He fell to the ground, curled up in pain. She dragged him to the sidewalk. Susanna jumped into the truck then. She sideswiped the patrol car and lurched east on West Central, accelerating fast.

That was when she must have seen something in the intersection. Tony said it was a woman pushing a stroller. But he's a sentimental kind of guy. I didn't see anything. I was too busy hanging on to Greg. I figured it was one of the cops from a second car that turned up.

Mark said it was a couple walking hand in hand. Susanna swerved to avoid what-ever it was. She can't have noticed the huge

SUV heading into the intersection, speeding west. She ploughed head-on into it.

She wasn't wearing a seatbelt.

* * *

"Thanks for your help," I said to Mark Davies, shaking his hand.

I wasn't sure I meant it. He still seemed much too interested in Angela. And I had serious plans for change and reform in that direction.

"I appreciate your help too," he said. "You've saved us money and a lot of embarrassment."

"How?" I said. "You'll pardon my asking, sir, but who are you?"

Angela burst into laughter. "Really, Rick. Didn't you know? He's my boss," she said. "Remember? I have a new job."

"What exactly do you do?" I asked her.

"I work for an insurance company," said Angela. "Imperial and Northern. Investigating fraud."

"And she's very good at it," said Mark. "I'm here because Cheryl was insured with us. But I wanted to talk to you anyway. And I appreciated being able to watch you work. Angela's told me a lot about you."

"She has?"

"Yes. We need another investigator. It would be good to have someone on the team who speaks Spanish."

He took a business card from his pocket. "Think about it. Call me if you're interested."

CHAPTER TWENTY-ONE

ANGELA: ONCE MORE

The business of giving statements had taken the better part of the afternoon.

They let me observe Greg's interview. It was interesting.

"I never wanted to have anything to do with it," he said. "I loved her and I just wanted to marry her. I told her I was making enough money for both of us. She could have quit work if she wanted. But this guy had offered her a lot of money if she would help him out. And to do it, she needed my truck."

"What did she want you to do?"

"Drive over to the jail on Friday morning," he said.

"That's it? Just drive over to the jail."

"We met this guy. Paco. He was there to pick up a friend who had no place to stay. So Susanna was going to let him have Rick's apartment. Just until he found his own place."

"Was this person Fred Hancock?"

"They called him Freddie. No one ever told me his last name. He seemed scared to death. He climbed in the back. We went and picked up groceries and took him to Susanna's house. Cheryl was at work."

"Tell us about Wednesday."

"I picked her up at noon from work," he said in a low voice. "We met this Paco again. He picked up some stuff and put it in the back of the truck. We drove to Susanna's place. Cheryl was home, and Susanna made us all some lunch. Except Paco. He went down to see Freddie. Cheryl got really sleepy, and we helped her to bed…"

He started to sob. After several minutes of that, the interview was terminated.

I left feeling sick.

* * *

Now I was standing in the living room of Angela's apartment. I was not sure what to do next. Until these last three days, Angela and I hadn't seen each other since May. That night in May, we had gone out for dinner to talk things over. The lighting in the restaurant was suitably romantic. I ordered a bottle of wine. The music was soft and the food and wine were good. We went back to my apartment. We had decided to give our marriage another chance.

It didn't work. I was in a foul temper in the morning. I had a headache from too much wine. And we fought. They were the same fights about the same things. Like the ones we had before she threw me out. That was when I decided to leave for the farm. Now I was standing under a bright light in the middle of the room. Angela was looking out the window.

"What do you think?" she asked.

"About what?"

"About the job with Imperial. What did you think I meant?"

"I didn't know," I said. "It was a real coincidence that Cheryl was insured with your boss's company, wasn't it?"

"Not really," said Angela. "Like he said, they were friends. She was the one who told me he was looking for another investigator. Poor guy. He was really upset about her death."

"He seems to be nice."

"He is," said Angela. "I like him a lot."

I had a cold feeling in the pit of my stomach just thinking of him and Angela. He was probably neat. And never got drunk and said stupid things he didn't mean.

"Look. I'd better go. You must be tired. It's been a really long day."

"I think there's food in the refrigerator.

Let's make supper. Unless you really want to get out of here."

There was no answer to that.

* * *

"Sit down," she said. We had eaten and talked about everything and nothing. We had cleaned up the kitchen. Angela seemed in a good mood. "I thought we should celebrate another success," she said. "Just a minute."

She came back with a beer and two glasses.

"Is this a test?" I asked.

"Sort of," she said, pouring out the beer.

She sat down on the couch. I was in a big chair across from her.

"What did you call me about?" I asked. "I don't know what happened to your message. I'm really sorry. I got other messages, so I thought the machine was working okay."

"Susanna probably checked out your messages. She must have deleted the ones she didn't want you to get."

"Maybe," I said. "She always snooped around. What was it about? The case?"

"No," she said. "I wanted to let you know…" She stared out the window and shook her head. As if she couldn't get the words out.

"What?" I had to find out. "You wanted to tell me you were involved with someone else?"

"Don't be stupid, Rick," she said angrily. "I wanted you to know that I was pregnant. But it didn't matter. I lost the baby. That was my second message." Her voice was bitter and unhappy. "So you don't have to worry about it."

I left the chair. I crouched down in front of her and grabbed her hands. "My god, Angela. I swear I didn't know. That's why you fixed up the junk room."

"Yes, that's why."

"That bitch! I would have come right back. As soon as I got the first message. I would have."

"Maybe someone else erased the message," said Angela.

"It had to be Susanna," I said. "She had a set of keys. She could get in the apartment whenever she wanted. And she didn't want me back too soon."

"And she knew you," said Angela. "She knew you would come back. That's what bothered me. I knew you would too. I needed you." Tears spilled down her cheeks.

I stood up and pulled her close.

"I'm here, Angela. Kind of late, but I'm here."

I held her tight until the tears stopped.

"Maybe I shouldn't leave you alone tonight after all," I said. "I'll sleep on the couch. We can talk in the morning."

"Don't be stupid," she said. "We have a perfectly good bed. And after all, we're still married, aren't we?"

I turned off the lights and followed her into our bedroom.

Mystery writer CAROLINE MEDORA
SALE ROE is the author of fourteen novels.
As Medora Sale, she has written six police
procedurals, including *Murder on the Run*,
winner of an Arthur Ellis Award for best
first novel. The author is a past president of
both the international organization Sisters
in Crime and the Crime Writers of Canada.
She lives with her husband in Toronto.